PERSEPHONE ON THE METRO

Wendy Taylor Carlisle

MadHat Press
Asheville, North Carolina

MadHat Press
MadHat Incorporated
PO Box 8364, Asheville, NC 28814

ISBN 978-1-941196-03-8 (paperback)

Book and cover design by MadHat Press

www.madhat-press.com

FIFTH LABOR

If you want a different story, you swing
the mop. What I remember is the weight

> of nights and their particulars, sunrise
> as a mist before the day slid over us,

lifting like an indigo balloon, striped
to amuse the limbic part of the brain that

> sees a lover through the window, gone up
> the gravel path with the noble rattle and

crunch of a serious journey, his canteen
swaying. But for me there's something prissy

> about talking like this without mentioning
> dirt and residue, listing the leftovers:

greasy knife, stained linens—when I know later
if I want the place clean, I move the river.

CONTENTS

IRONING WITH ZEUS

There is no iron, just the periodic flash,
the sizzled-smell of dampened wool. As Ops

         taught him, he starts at the neck and when he's done,
         he stacks the folded tunics in his small workroom,

in the dusty Department of Theology, his
whole world now. He never steps outside to listen
for the wind's echo, or check the river bank for swans.

         If he misses a panel or sears a collar,
         this lapse, caused by his errant company— bull, bear,
         heifer, gold coin shower— engages his quest for

a more perfect crease. His lusts now are Faultless,
are to press the wrinkles from that other life. He wishes

         not to recall the former, steamy him. He shuns
         the wrinkled, the rumpled, the Olympian.

MAKING THE BED WITH ARIADNE

i.

Naturally, being a princess, she objects
to cotton sheets— their crisp whiteness suggests

> passing into, not out of, sleep's blind alley,
> but once she undertakes to solve the mystery

of tuck and reverse, she shapes each hospital
corner square as a bull's stall, unwinds ruffled

> eyelet to expose the comforter's
> dark center. This Ariadne's a match for

any household chore. Even the Blu-ray bellowing
downstairs can't keep order from unrolling

> under her fingers as she toils her way
> through tangled hours, spooling down every

corridor, threading through the chambers' maze,
ordering disorder, shifting dimness into day.

ii.

According to Minos, her bullish dad,
Efficient Ariadne made her bed

       & if the sheets chafed when she woke, then *tough*.
           She had been, he said, *too clever by half*

with her waiting boat, her twine. Unhappy child,
sleep took her like a storm of bees, shut her eyes

           with hymenopterous lullabies, *You snooze*
          you lose, her father roared, *don't whine.* That dad

who butchered virgins, fourteen at a whack,
got furious. Rebellion in his bashful

          daughter gave him a chance to sneer *I warned her*
           off good looking men, and just as he fore-

cast, on Naxos, Theseus had a plan,
as bullish as her dad, he sailed, was gone.

Col. Tom Parker at the Pearly Gates

Before he had a hit I saw it, something
busted in his face. But I confess his image

> was my thing, his heartbreak, blue suede, how he loved
> his ma, his swivel hips—all mine. The public

knows so much these days but you recall how silent
stars were then, how shrewd about their drugs and crimes.

> Yeah, I confess I gave him speed when he wore out.
> He scored that morphine on his own. That was a shock.

I meant to keep him on the Vegas strip for years
and could have if he took the cure. I will declare

> he had an ache. It showed up when he'd pose for fans—
> how he'd romance them—walk his baby girl down

to the end of Graceland's lawn just to hear them
people, back behind the fence, keening like wind.

HOME FIRES

At the gates, Peleus' boy, the one with the bad
heel, waits. The Gods know, his mother tried

> to save him, to make her mixed marriage last.
> Six children sacrificed, the ardent goddess

blazed to purge her seventh of mortality
but where she held him, he scalded.

> Out of childhood's shadow, he doesn't feel
> his own weak foot; he can't recall

the water or the stranger's bone. Still, eager
for vengeance, not enticed to live forever out of the river

> he hefts the great round shield, his principal defense
> his mother's love. Underneath his breastplate

what is mortal and almost mortal thrums.
He doesn't notice how the touched place burns.

PERSEPHONE ON THE METRO

i.
She rushes down the stairs. Her mother shouts,
In gods' names, don't be gone all night. She barely
hears. She's trying not to trip on narrow stairs
or drown in streams of *hommes et femmes* that sluice down

                  to the tracks, as if the Metro were a river
                    of desire they were called to enter, just

the moment that a perfect car arrived. She
slumps onto a wooden bench beside an *au pair*

                  rocking someone else's baby on her hip,
              she yawns at undergrads dressed down in Gap,

ignores the buzzed-up business dudes. She sees
the locals know how to descend to get

around les avenues below. To her,
this foreign underground is all fresh news.

ii.

Under *la rue* she slows; she reads the news,
spells out ads for cheap *vacance*, the film reviews.

She mouths directions to herself, reruns
the strange name of her stop. Her train shrieks up.

      She slides inside the door, does not look back—
      one quick glance for the inmates of her car—

baguettes in men's arms, dogs in women's laps,
a clutch of squirmless teens, beguiled it seems,

      by a grim stranger on her left. Curious,
      she turns to him but even vis-à-vis

such darkness, doesn't flinch. What did her mom
call to her as she left? Graffitied walls scream

past. At Reuilly-Diderot, the stranger snares
her wrist, pulls her to his unearthly stair—
        and down

SECOND LABOR

Today my friend described the tree house in her dream,
the one with the windows that wouldn't close
and it reminded me of a stucco house we lived in when the boys
were in high school—the place that had Safeway cartons

nailed to the studs and wallpapered over. In November
there was ice on the inside of the windows and my youngest lost
his boa down the toilet. When the caretaker tried to molest
the oldest boy, we got the jump on him. Under pressure,

the three of us worked well together. There were nine kinds
of problems in that place. When we solved one, there came another.
We moved when the pipe broke and sewage leaked

down the drive and under the wheels of the Volkswagen
my mother-in-law got us out of guilt because her son vanished
and left us carless. We were on fire. The snake never came back.

JONAH

I'm always out of place, standing at the edge of parties,
breathing quietly, trying to look as if I belonged with some
group of strangers who believe in praying eleven times a day,
that an orgasm can be delayed indefinitely or even that Jonah
dwelt for seventy-two hours in the belly of the leviathan, which
was probably a sperm whale with a whale's colossal head and
room enough inside for him and his carpet bag with the extra
cape he packed in case the weather turned off cold in Joppa,
which was where he was headed until he ran into that fish.

Later, Jonah discovered Yahweh doesn't withhold His mercy,
even from a beached sailor, even from the party people in
Nineveh. This saved the prophet, may have even comforted
him, but it doesn't relieve me much as I peer into this cocktail
party full of Assyrians, people who should know better, people
who tonight will each have at least three drinks and get up late
tomorrow and not remember my name or the names of my
gods but drive to work and Target and never notice a stranger or
look up at the sky and never ever think of taking an unexpected
ride.

THE WOUND

And one of them smote the servant of the high priest, and cut off his right ear. And Jesus answered and said, Suffer ye thus far. And he touched his ear, and healed him.
                    Luke 22: 50-51

Was it good or bad
Luck to be Malchus,

To stand close enough
To take the first cut

At the end of that
Story? Was he dumb-

Struck by half-silence
As his deaf ear lay

In the dust, curling
Toward paradise? Did

He consider how,
In an instant, we

Can leave one fate for
Another? Or did

He overhear the
Fearful whispers, but

Remain untouched, back
Away, vanish in-

to the heedless crowd?

SPEAKING IN TONGUES

... when he said to them, "Did you receive the Holy Spirit...?" They replied, "No, we have not even heard there is a Holy Spirit." ... Paul laid his hand upon their heads and the Holy Spirit came upon them and they spoke in tongues..."...

Acts 19:1-6

Satisfied
without Him.
Not talking
about a
visit. Not
speaking of
anything,
really. Not
knowing what
to respond
because we
hadn't heard
the question
before, or
imagined
an answer.
Not certain
Spirit was
anything
to us. We
began to
speak as most
people do
and were stunned
to find in
gibberish

meaning, for
those in need
of meaning,
miracles
for the rest.

I, DOVE

Torn from the heavens—
the heavens torn—
but descending softly as a small gray bird, light

as a pinfeather
            I am well-pleased
how often have you wanted to hear

those words not splintered
like the fisted garage door or accidentally
caught running down the alley

by a heavy hand, not ripped like the shirt
off your sweating shoulders,
torn like the sky

when you wanted to be set free,
when your need to please
was as far away from your capacity

as heaven's farthest galaxy, when
you knew finally
there would be more struggle,

would be pain incarnate,
appalling enough to drive you into a wilderness,

that you would become
as a wild beast, tempted,
that you would never see

the angels all around you—
never until the end
        embrace the good news.

HONEY

Stones came at her like bees to candy/ And sweet redheaded harlot that she was/
She screamed out, "I never, I never."

Anne Sexton

The redhead is losing what she never owned,
a man's hands, those curious bears,
the ravaged plane of his chest, his skin,
its pores and wrinkles, his strange, familiar
smell, the beehive of his shivering.
I never—

The redhead's peaceful days disappear.
She turns for comfort to honey, to mayfly, to river,
considers the invisible inverse—
a cooler universe where her neighbors
would love her and bless desire.
Avoiding their eyes, she backs away.

Over her shoulder, the first rock—
she bends to pick it up—
                              I never. We never. Never—

I Swan

Everyone makes much of it but truth to tell
the honor could have had more physical appeal
trumpeters have limited romantic skills
and lack imagination, not to mention lips.

During the act, I must admit, I entertained
some questions of a theologic nature.
The poets say he overwhelmed me on that bank—
a sudden blow, the storms of wings.

Why do they reckon I gave in? Inquisitive. You bet.
And let me say that even mediocre sex
can't take the edge off having done it with a God.

As for the kids, around the neighborhood
my alibi is this: they came from eggs.
Don't blame me if they didn't turn out good.

PENELOPE

Getting older with each day's shuttle and not one
moment's peace, just push and hustle. My most pliant

        part's my hands, I guess from lanolin. O Sweet
        Minerva, give me a new prank, a bluff to keep

the suitors' hands off, keep 'em pacified. When some
Procis runs an eager palm against my thigh, I

        all but jump out of my dress. But I sit quiet,
        clasp the family honor close while they prize me loud

and raucous, chiefly for my real estate. How could
I slap the mattress with some brazen hunk, although

        his chest is smooth and taut, with my Odysseus
        so good in bed? I think I recall that. Men whisper

I have magic, a loom that undoes daylight's doing,
but they aren't there when I unravel, tear night loose.

To Paris, Love Oenone

It's just an apple, you said, and lobbed it.
That was after you left us, the boy and me
and claimed it was your mother's gaffe caused all

                that fuss over the Golden Delicious.
          "For the Fairest," you said, chose a goddess.
      Of course, from three lame bribes, you favored lust

How fast you fell and then how little time
had passed before you blamed the gods, the fates,
the moon. Worse than your war is me here on this

             mountain with its famous wind, imagining
                 a claret sea, your fingers run amok
              in her gold hair. Promised the loveliest,

you got what was coming to a hound.
I pulled my hand back, never touched your wound.

WHAT WAS IT TO SNOW WHITE?

The shape of the mirror
    a walk in the woods
        the homecoming

rendered in miniature
    seven little stories
        like the nip of conscience?

Her trade-off for three hots & a cot—
    polish fourteen boots,
        furbish one sideboard, pull

seven custodial twelves, tangled
    in brooms and dishrags
        end up exhausted, ravenous.

For a Rome Beauty then
    it was nothing
        to open the door.

Glass-encased, what mattered
    after ever after but that apple,
        his kisses, the cost of the fruit.

WOLF

It is not hunger or its empty bowl
He fears. It's a helpless taste for pork that drives

And masters him— hog lust eating up the night,
Chewing through the dark to their tidy houses.

Straw, then sticks, then brick, he admires
The walls, imagines them blown away, razed,

Pictures pig families lighting lamps,
Telling tales, bearing young. He craves them

Skewered, bar-b-qued, to ease his fearful
Appetite. At night, he tells himself

That sows are born fools, that pigs exist
To tempt a wolf. He is a fiend to get at them.

Will chance the steep climb to the chimney
To catch the smell of rank, sweet hides:

Useless swine, porkers, prey. He'll slide
To their hot center, their hot, sweet center.

after Andrea Hollander Budy

CARY GRANT'S FACE

In the photo from the '59 festival he looks out over
Kim Novak's shoulder, her back a heart, bound
in perfect black velvet over a spread of tulle.

Gleaming at me from the magazine that morning, they
embodied all mid-century bromides on the uses of beauty,
on a woman's duty to be smiling,

wide-eyed, solicitous of her man. From Cannes
that year came the proof— Cary remade,
immersed, besotted, rendered docile by passion.

You could see it plain in his 8X10, just as it was when
he floated high on the wall of our gym
with Elizabeth Taylor and James Dean, three deities

to decorate a tenth-grade prom, where adolescent, awkward,
we sweated into rented tuxes and party dresses. And I,
with my new breasts torpedoed out, my waist defined by

plastic bones, fox trotted and tried to remember what I'd heard
about boys: what made them like you, what made them
act nice, "Be Pretty." "Be silent." "Don't beat them at tennis,"

were the lines I recalled as I dodged the Spanish moss,
my crinoline dusting the hard wood, the rest of Mom's coaching
displaced, in my mind that other fête,

Kim's platinum back, her boyfriend smiling over her as if
she'd created him flawless, dreamed him into a gentleman, as if
she knew just what to say to make him a star.

X FILES

It's taken some time but I really like his looks, the guy from the X files with the Slavic bone structure and the episode I'm watching is the one where some chubby-faced guy with the nondescript physique, a schmuck really, has fathered five children by five different women because he could change his anatomy whenever he wanted. It's all done subQ in the muscle layer, unconvincing but enticing. To make the story short, he can shapeshift and today he's become the hero-guy with the razorblade cheekbones, who I really like looking at now after years of seeing his face each week and on reruns and who I know will eventually catch this mutant creep while all of us stare, move our eyebrows up and down, suck in our chops, purse our mouths and try to morph our faces into more angular faces or manufacture the wet bee-stung lips so popular now.

Darling, you say, desire depends on what you're used to, where you were born. But for me, it's more what's on each week in syndication, a televised ecstasy lights up my small-screen—although I know a chiseled cheek, some pale reflected skin, in short, love as telecast, will not transfigure Mister X or us.

Wendy Taylor Carlisle

How Could Norma Jean

be one more high school angel, unnoticed
in the back row, not enrolled in pliant blond, once

                she had found the appetite in new-milk skin
        and that proficiency in thrown-back head and arms akimbo?

She had to amplify on schoolgirl, ingénue.
And wouldn't you agree to alter and become that Playmate,

         skirt blown north? Virtue never flashed so white a smile.
        O Marilyn, your fleshy thighs, that waist

that celebrates the absolute, the cinched-in,
that glow that ripens and festers in Technicolor.

         How could you not stay on at the party, sleepily crooning
        Happy Birthday, sewn into that impossible gown?

Out on the rim of self-invention, Norma teases us one screen farther
becomes at The End an eloquent flicker, indistinct in black and white.

NOTES

page v: The Fifth Labor of Hercules was to clean the Augean Stable.

page 1: The god Zeus was notorious for his changeable love life: he turned Callisto into a bear, Io a white heifer. Zeus himself became a bull and a swan and, for Danae, he became a shower of gold coins.

page 8: The Second labor of Hercules was to kill the Lernaean Hydra, a many-headed serpent-like beast.

page 18: Paris' first love was the nymph, Oenone. He left her for Helen and Troy.

ACKNOWLEDGMENTS

For David

With thanks to the journals that published these poems in one form or another: *2River View, Alba, Aquila Review, fieralingue, Meridian, Munyori, Perihelion, poetrymagazine.com, Salt River Review, Story South,* the *Sound, Unlikely Stories, Windhover,* and *znine*

And to the poets who helped the Gods along: Pam, Selena, Margo, Tamam, to my ever-patient editor, Jonathan, and as always, to Phil & his poetry factory.

ABOUT THE AUTHOR

Wendy Taylor Carlisle lives in the spaces between Texas and Arkansas, Arkansas and Missouri, Texas and Louisiana. She is the author of two books, *Discount Fireworks* (Jacaranda Books 2008) and *Reading Berryman to the Dog* (Jacaranda Books, 2000) and two chapbooks, *After Happily Ever After*, (2River Chapbook Series, #15) and *The Storage of Angels* (Slow Water Press, 2008).

www.ingramcontent.com/pod-product-compliance
Lightning Source LLC
Chambersburg PA
CBHW050919120626
46552CB00004B/1660